A Farmyard Christmas Concert

To all those parents whose children
never practise their instruments

First published 2010

Copyright © 2010 Sam Cooper

Published by THINGLEY PRESS, Corsham, Wiltshire

ISBN 978-0-9566118-1-9

Illustrations by Hermione Skrine

Design and origination by Phill Zillwood

Santa Claus stood at
the front of the barn.
He raised the baton
with a flick of his arm.

The cats on their fiddles
obediently played –
What glorious music their
violins made!

Santa Claus listened but
then shook his head.

*"It's good, but it
still can be better,"*

he said.

He pulled out his whistle
and gave a shrill squeak
And the dogs all responded,
from bloodhound to peke.

Each picked up his cello
and flourished his bow
And the string section tuned up
from high down to low.

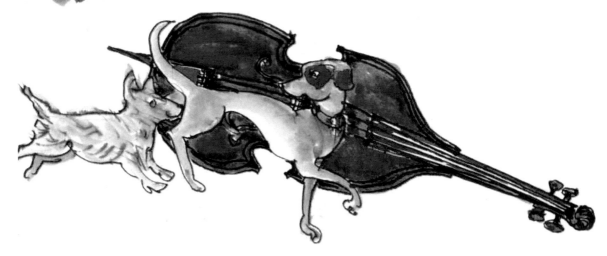

Santa Claus listened but
then shook his head.

"*It's good, but it
still can be better,*"
he said.

He whistled. The woodwind
arrived on the wing.
The cooing of doves made
the clarinets sing.

On oboes were ducks, on
flutes nightingales,
And the tiniest wren trilled
the piccolo's scales.

Santa Claus listened but
then shook his head.

*"It's good, but it
still can be better,"*
he said.

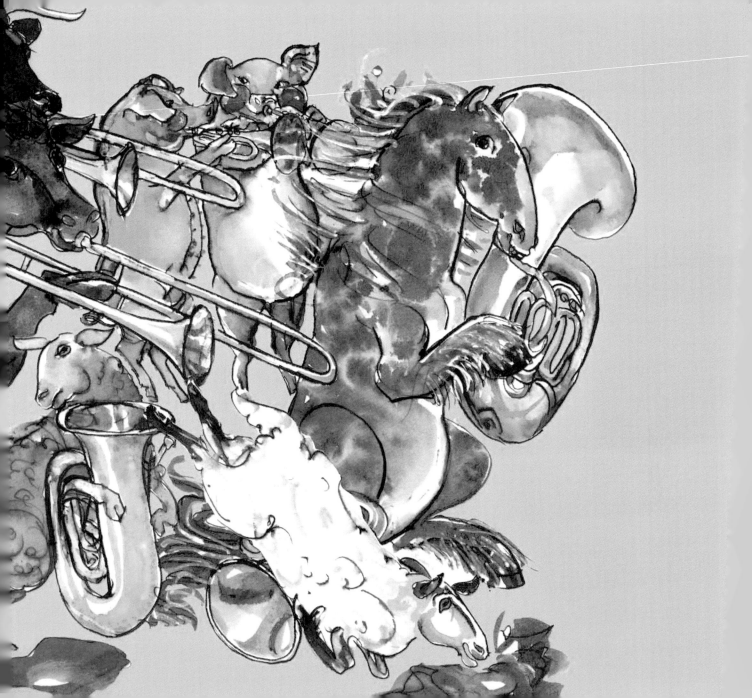

He whistled. The farmyard
was suddenly quiet,
But in the brass section
was nearly a riot -

The pigs on the trumpets,
the cows on trombone,
The carthorse on tuba,
the sheep on euphon - (ium).

Santa Claus listened but then shook his head.
"*It's good, but it still can be better,*" he said.

He whistled.
The countryside
hurried to come.
The rabbit's back
legs thumped a
beat on the drum.

The mice swung on cymbals, the fox struck the gong,
And the might of percussion was joined to the throng.

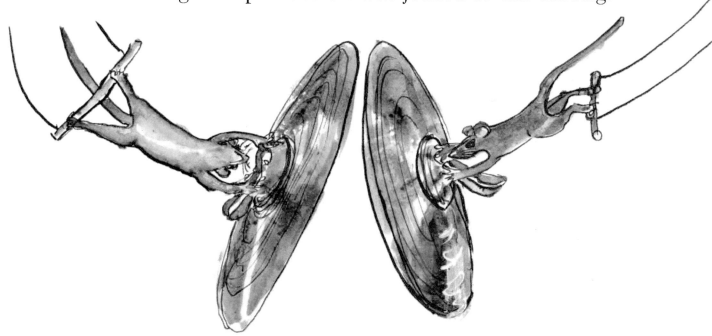

Santa Claus listened but then shook his head.
"*It's good, but it still can be better,*"he said.

The hedgehog's young
daughter was painfully shy.
She snuffled and shuffled
to catch Santa's eye,

Not quite daring to ask if
she might have her turn
On a hedgehog-sized
instrument, easy to learn.

And when Santa noticed
her, he was inspired -
He realised then just what
his band still required.

The sweep of the strings and the xylophone's jangle

Still needed the voice
of the humble triangle!

The hedgehog was given
her own little score
And taught how to count
to bar seventy-four,

And then – in a pause in
the orchestra's sound –
The "ting" of the triangle
tinkled around.

Santa Claus listened and
nodded his head...

"It's perfect, it couldn't be better," he said.